THE GREAT ICE CREAM WAR OF SUMMER 2016

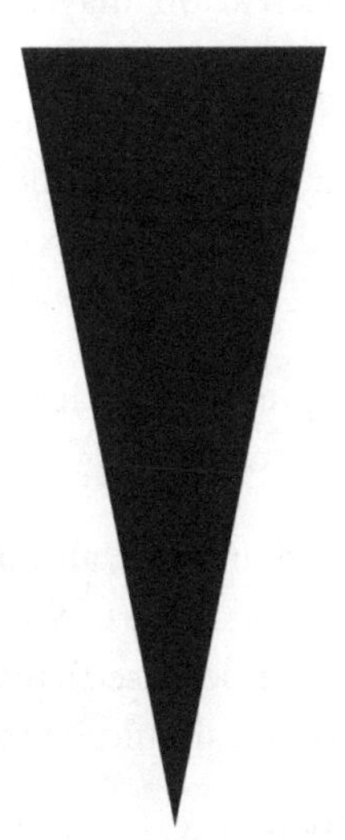

JOHN A. BROCK

The morning hours, before the ice cream shop opened, were Ted's favorite part of the day.

Clipboard in hand, he stood in the freezer taking inventory in the dim light, the hum of the motors and the cool air a welcome relief from the brutal heat that summer had unleashed on the town. The ritual always brought a sting of nostalgia in memories of watching his father perform the same weekly task. As he was lost in thought, the clanging of the shopkeeper's bell echoed down the hallway and through the open freezer door.

"Can't anyone read anymore?" Ted grumbled. It wasn't yet ten, and he couldn't imagine anyone so impatient for ice cream this early in the day. He heard Sophie welcome the visitor as he set his clipboard down on a barrel of Rocky Road, wiping his hands on his apron before stepping out and shutting the freezer door behind him.

"We're closed," Ted called out as he walked down the hallway.

A tall, rail-thin young man with a shaggy dark beard and black-framed glasses stood on the checkerboard tile and offered a wide smile. "Sorry, I can come back later."

"Nonsense," Sophie said from behind the counter. "Have a cup of coffee with us."

"That sounds great."

Sophie smiled, then turned to Ted with a slight nod of her head.

"Ted Stroud," he said and offered his hand. "And this is my wife, Sophie."

The man took his hand with a firm grip. His sleeves were rolled up to his elbows, and Ted shot a glance at the colorful tattoos that ran down his forearms. The man's beard and glasses failed to hide his youth, his eyes bright and beaming. "Nice to meet both of you. I'm Brad Wilkinson." He released his grip and surveyed the dining room. "You have a great place here. I love all this retro stuff."

A dozen small lime-green tables and padded metal chairs filled the room, a throwback to the fifties. Lining the walls, framed photographs chronicled the shop's history, from opening day through birthday parties and major events over its forty years of business. Large glass windows gave a splendid view of the park across the street, and in the back corner stood a jukebox full of classic records.

"We had an ice cream place just like this where I grew up," Brad said.

"I guess there's a shop like this anywhere you go," Ted said. "Are you passing through?" The town of Howell was almost in the center of Texas and fifteen miles from the interstate that could take you either southeast to San Antonio or northwest to Amarillo. Most visitors either stopped for a quick visit for some small-town charm or had taken a wrong turn off the highway.

"No, we just moved here." Brad walked over to

the jukebox and studied the song selections. "Buddy Holly, Chuck Berry, Roy Orbison. You even have Elvis!"

"Only the best."

"Vinyl records are making a comeback, you know. You might be sitting on a small fortune here. But I don't see any Beatles?"

"My father didn't care for them much. I was born in the seventies, so I was more into Billy Joel, the Eagles, Fleetwood Mac. But my folks only allowed songs from the fifties in the jukebox."

Sophie carried a small tray with three coffee cups and set it down on one of the light green Formica tables as Ted took a seat. Brad took one last look at the jukebox and walked over, scraping the chair against the tile in a fashion that Ted knew irritated his wife before sitting down.

"Cream? Sugar?" Sophie asked.

"Black's fine with me." Brad lifted the cup and took a careful sip, a grin breaking across his face. "Now I know where I'm getting my morning coffee. That's very good."

Sophie took a seat across from Brad and cradled her cup. "What brings you to our town?"

"Had to get out of the big city," Brad said and took another sip. "We're from Denver. Very nice, but very expensive. Competition for jobs got tough, and to be honest, we got tired of the winters."

"I noticed your wedding band."

"Three years now. My wife's name is Rita. She wanted to scour the antique store for some stuff for the new house. I don't have the patience for that kind of thing, so I decided to look around downtown a bit. That's how I found your shop."

Sophie nodded. "Well, we're glad you found us."

"May I ask what line of work you're in?" Ted asked.

Brad carefully set his cup down. "This summer I plan on starting a new business. Something new for both Rita and me. Have either of you heard of gelato?"

Sophie placed an arm on Ted's arm. "Sure. Howell may be a small town, but we've heard that term before."

"Of course," Brad said. "I'm used to having to explain to my parents that it's basically Italian ice cream."

Ted and Sophie exchanged a quick glance, wondering if equating their presumed age with that of his parents was intentional. Brad took another sip of his coffee, letting the silence hover over the table.

"So, you're our new competition?" Sophie said.

"Oh, competition is too strong of a word, I think. Our business model is quite different than your brick-and-mortar shop. We'll be selling our product from a different location day to day."

Ted crossed his arms against his chest. "Like an ice cream truck?"

Brad eyes lit up, eager to explain. "Not in the traditional sense. We won't be driving up and down the street all day, playing that annoying song over and over to sell two-dollar popsicles."

"Do you mean like a food truck?" Sophie asked.

"Exactly. Wherever there's a crowd, we'll try to be there. We store and sell everything from our truck. We already have a date set next weekend at the parking lot of the hardware store. Hopefully we'll get some business, being so close to the highway and all."

"Frank's going to let you sell ice cream?" A friend since grade school, Ted knew Frank to be very conservative when it came to his store. The thought of letting a truck on his property without cutting him in on the profits seemed unbelievable.

"Gelato. I explained that our truck could help bring in some customers for him. He seems to be struggling with that superstore opening a few miles down the road."

Brad described his business in more detail and reassured them that he didn't view them as competitors. Even though both Ted and Sophie knew they were being fed a line, the young man's smooth and mannered speech made him impossible to dislike.

In turn, Ted briefly recounted the history of Stroud's Ice Cream Shop, from its grand opening in the early 1980s to his strict father's unexpected passing fourteen years before, and how Ted took over the shop. Brad spoke about being raised by an Air Force father and a strict stay-at-home mother in Colorado. Both men agreed that the discipline instilled in them at a young age was the greatest gift they received from their parents.

"Let me show you a picture of my wife." Brad pulled out his wallet and flipped it open to a photo of a striking-looking woman with sleek red hair and dark eyes with a smile as wide as the sky.

"Stunning," Sophie said as Ted nodded in agreement.

"She's the best," Brad said as he folded the wallet and stuffed it into his back jeans pocket. "We named the business after her: the Lovely Rita."

Sophie stood and grabbed the carafe of coffee off the counter, offering Brad a refill.

"I better not, I get a bit on edge if I have too much caffeine. Besides, I better find Rita. We just closed on a house, and she may have bought enough furniture for two by now."

"Congratulations," Ted said.

"What part of town?" Sophie asked. "We may be neighbors."

"It's a new development out west of town near the highway. I should remember the name of the neighborhood, something like North Point?"

"North Ridge," Sophie said with a smile.

"Yes, that's it. Thank you."

Sophie refilled Ted's cup. "It's out by the lake

where the new movie theater's at."

"Oh, sure," Ted said, vaguely remembering driving by the new houses on their date night a few weeks ago. He couldn't even remember what the movie was about, having lost interest in much of what popular culture found entertaining, but Sophie enjoyed it.

"The theater was one of the main selling points," Brad said. "In Denver, you had to drive thirty minutes and pay for parking to see one. From our house, we can just walk. And our new place is so much bigger, it's amazing how cheap houses are in Texas."

Ted gave Sophie a quick glance as he took a sip of coffee. With their rising property taxes making their mortgage payments more of a struggle, housing didn't seem very cheap to him.

"I think you'll like living in our little town," Sophie said. "No traffic, warm weather for the most part. Friendly people."

"For the most part," Ted said with a grin. "We'll give you a list of the folks to avoid."

"If everyone is half as nice as both of you, we'll be delighted." Brad said. "Thanks for the coffee, and I'm sure we'll be seeing a lot of each other."

Brad scraped his chair back along the floor and stood, shaking hands with both of them before walking to the door and stepping out into the bright morning sunshine. Ted and Sophie took another sip of coffee before speaking.

"Nice guy," Ted said.

Sophie set her cup down. "Soft hands, not used to hard work. And how could he afford a house in North Ridge at his age? His parents must be well off."

"I didn't get that sense about him," Ted said.

"Because you don't pay attention," Sophie said sweetly but firmly.

"What other signals did I miss?"

Sophie nodded at the coffee cup Brad left at the table. "If he would've picked up his cup and walked toward the sink, I would've happily told him to let me rinse out his cup. But he leaves it there and walks out the door like I'm his maid or something."

"You're reading too much into this," Ted said with a chuckle.

"Am I now?" Sophie suddenly stood and dramatically scraped her chair across the tile. "You didn't hear that?" She repeated the annoying screech by pushing the chair back and forth across the floor.

Ted shook his head as she picked up Brad's cup. "Here, take my cup since you're heading that way."

Sophie smiled. "Young or old, you men are all the same. I don't know why we put up with all of y'all." She took Ted's cup and walked toward the sink behind the counter.

"Might as well open up," Ted said. He stood up and stretched.

"Why not? Shame to keep all our customers

waiting."

Ted never loved his wife more than when she was sarcastic. He walked to the glass door, took a deep breath, and turned the hanging sign from closed to open.

The two childhood friends listened to the band as they struggled through a classic country song. Ted picked at his beer coaster like a scab, and it wasn't until near the end of the song that Ted recognized it. The crowd, more interested in their drinks, gave them a light smatter of applause as the band announced they were taking a short break.

"So, he doesn't pay you or anything?" Ted asked.

"Why?" Frank poured himself another beer from the pitcher. "I should pay him for bringing in the customers like he did."

Frank had suffered a run of bad luck in recent years. His wife had had a health scare, and though it ended up being nothing serious, the medical tests and doctor visits had taken a big chunk of their savings. His son George moved back home after being laid off from the oil field. Ted had a soft spot for George, who had dated his daughter Emma through high school. For Emma, the relationship wasn't serious, and when she gently broke up with him during the summer before she left for college, George was shattered. Now he spent most of his days working for his father at the hardware store.

"They parked their truck right off the highway," Frank continued. "Anyone driving by couldn't help but notice all those bright hippie colors. What do you call it?"

"Psychedelic," Ted said.

"Yeah, like those shirts at Woodstock. Half an hour after they set up, they had a line of folks waiting. Stayed that way most of the day."

"But did it help your store? Did customers come in and buy stuff?"

"Here and there," Frank said, shifting in his chair. "Most people came for the ice cream."

"Gelato," Ted corrected him.

"Right. But I did see some new faces walk in. Bought little things like duct tape, nails, whatever. I did sell a high-end grill that's been sitting there a while, but that was a regular customer so not sure I could give them credit for that."

Frank picked up the pitcher, filled Ted's glass with the remaining beer, and held it up to catch the waitress's attention.

"Didn't help my bottom line much, but it felt good being noticed. Most of the time I sit there watching the cars speed down the highway. At least a few of those cars stopped for a minute or two."

The waitress smiled and whisked the pitcher from Frank's hand. She looked vaguely familiar, and when

Ted noticed the thin, crooked scar running down her left cheek he remembered her as a classmate of his daughter's. Though he missed Emma terribly, he felt a wave of gratitude that she had escaped before the town had dug its claws into her.

"This will have to be the last pitcher of the night," Frank said. "We're trying something new, opening at eight instead of ten. Early bird gets the worm and all that. With all the new housing going up on the edge of town, we're trying to get some of that construction money."

"Sophie says there's some high-priced development happening over there."

"Sure is. Everything is moving toward the highway. Soon our little town will be no more. Maybe you and I could open some kind of tourist trap, like a Bigfoot museum."

"We have no trees. Where would Bigfoot hide in our part of the world?"

"You were always the rational one, Ted."

The waitress came back with a cold pitcher of beer and set it down on the hardwood table. As they drank their last round of the night, their conversation turned to the chances of the local high school football team making the playoffs (not good), comparing their electricity bills with an uptick in summer rates, and their plans for the Fourth of July. The friends then turned quiet and listened to the band struggle through another song.

"How's Emma doing?" Frank asked when the song finished.

Ted smiled, always proud to talk about his daughter. "Good. She's taking summer classes so she won't have such a heavy schedule in the fall."

"Still planning on becoming a pharmacist?"

"I think so. She hasn't mentioned anything else to me, but Emma talks more to Sophie than to me about what's going in her life."

"Good profession to get into. Everyone seems to be on drugs nowadays. I bet Sophie's having a tough time with her little girl gone and having to take care of you."

Ted snickered. "She's doing alright. Emma's coming home for the Fourth, so that's not too far away." As soon as the words left his mouth, Ted wished he hadn't mentioned it. Frank might tell his son, who might mistake her visit as an opportunity to rekindle their relationship.

"All these years I'm still puzzled how you landed Sophie as a wife," Frank said with a slight slur in his speech, always a bit of a lightweight when it came to drinking. Ted felt relief it was his last glass of beer of the night.

"Right? I don't know how she's put up with me this long."

"All during high school, all the boys had a crush on her," Frank said and raised his hand. "This boy included."

Ted waved the waitress over as he pulled the wallet from his back pocket. When Frank started talking about their high school days, his mood would turn melancholic, and Ted was too tired to listen to such talk tonight. He placed a twenty and a ten on the table under the shaker of salt.

"Drinks are on me tonight," Ted said, waving to the waitress and pointing toward the bills. "I'll even throw in a free ride home."

"I'm fine," Frank said. "You don't have to do that."

"I've got some nice stinky cigars stashed away in the glove compartment that I need to get rid of. If Sophie finds them, I'll be in a world of trouble."

Ted stood and walked over next to Frank, ready to lend a hand if needed, but his friend stood up with no trouble. Together they weaved through the tables and chairs toward the exit door. Ted waited a moment to watch the waitress pick up the empty pitcher and stuff the cash into her pocket, then pushed the door open.

The two friends stepped outside into the darkness of the parking lot as a warm breeze swept over them. The gravel pebbles crackled with each step as they walked over to Ted's old Ford truck. Though in dire need of a coat of fresh paint, the truck had been reliable, and to Ted that was the only thing that mattered. He took his keys out of his pocket, unlocked the passenger door, and opened it for Frank. By the time Ted had climbed in the driver's side, Frank had opened the glove compartment and had a cigar ready for both.

"Cuban?" Frank asked as he passed one to Ted.

"Probably more like Oklahoma."

"Exotic," Frank said as he unwrapped his cigar.

The truck was old enough to have an ashtray under the radio, and Ted pulled it out, where a lighter lay waiting. He took the lighter and flicked the flame alive, bringing it to the tip of Frank's cigar. His friend took a couple of deep breaths until the tip glowed red, and then he exhaled a stream of smoke. Ted unwrapped and lit his own cigar before he started up the truck and pulled out of the parking lot.

The truck rumbled along the quiet street and the headlights stabbed through the darkness. The familiar sights they passed driving through the town were like looking through a dusty photo album of faded photographs. They passed the local grocery store where they both worked their first summer jobs, their elementary school whose brick exterior was now cracked and faded, and past the playground they played at as children, the empty swings swaying gently in the breeze.

The left headlight flickered a few times as Ted made a turn, then stopped. He'd meant to have the lights looked at, but with the beginning of summer he put it off. Now, though he knew he was far from intoxicated, he thought the flickering might catch the attention of a passing police car and worried a breathalyzer test might not agree.

They drove to the edge of town, enjoying their cigars. Strips of land that stood vacant for eternity were now torn and flattened. Skeletal wooden frames of future houses were scattered along the horizon, and the tires hummed smoothly along fresh-paved streets. The deeper they drove into the new developments, the more the roads weaved and turned.

"Could you slow down on those turns?" Frank asked, suddenly not looking well. "That last beer is catching up with me."

Ted nodded, slowing down as he took a circular turn around a cul-de-sac. The headlights swept across a wooden house frame where a group of darkened figures gathered around a fire burning in a steel barrel. The flames cast long shadows across the cement foundation, and several figures from the group turned toward the passing truck, lit cigarettes dangling from their mouths. They were only teenagers, and through the open window, he waved to them. The teenagers just stared.

Down another street, a few completed houses stood proudly. Lush green lawns soaked up the moonlight as flying bugs swirled around the glow of porch lights. Although far from being mansions, the houses stood tall as beacons of progress and prosperity for the small town.

"How can anyone afford a place like that?" Ted

said, but there was no reply. He turned to see that Frank had fallen asleep, his empty hand dangling outside the open window, the cigar having fallen somewhere along the way.

At the end of another cul-de-sac, Ted saw the bright colors of Brad's truck parked under the street-light with the words *Lovely Rita's Gelato* stenciled along the side. He gently stepped on the brakes, hoping not to wake his friend, but Frank shifted in his seat and opened his eyes.

"Home already?" he asked.

"Not yet." Ted parked behind the truck and placed his cigar in the ashtray. "I just want to take a quick look. You stay here."

Frank rubbed his eyes and looked toward the truck parked in front of the quiet house. "You think this is a good idea? They might think we're robbing them or something."

Ted opened his door and stepped out, keeping the engine running. "It's a public street. If someone sees us, we'll say we wanted to look around the new neighborhood."

He walked carefully toward the truck, studying the menu pasted by the ordering window. Though his shop carried a few flavors other than the standards, the flavors offered by the *Lovely Rita* were more exotic, such as tiramisu, stracciatella, cannoli, and raspberry brownie swirl, among others. The sizes were not large or small but *piccolo* and *grande*. But what really grabbed Ted's attention was the prices, almost double what his shop charged for a single scoop.

Ted ran his hand across the cool metal as he walked to the front. He wanted to peek inside, but the windshield was covered with a thick black curtain. Hoping there was a slight opening in the curtain where he could see the equipment, he gripped the driver's side door handle and pulled himself up to the running board. As soon as he gained his footing, an alarm shrieked loud enough to almost knock him off onto the street.

"What did you do?" Frank shouted through the open window, eyes darting back and forth in panic.

"Nothing," Ted said. He hopped off the running board and ran to the truck, quickly jumping in and shifting into drive.

The wheels spun to life. Ted maneuvered a quick U-turn around the cul-de-sac and as they passed the house they saw that the front door was open. Ted pressed the pedal to the floor as the engine rumbled in agony.

"I think they saw us," Frank said.

"We didn't do anything wrong."

"Then why are you driving like we robbed a bank?" Frank brought his hand to his chest. "You're going to give me a heart attack."

The truck sped down the neighborhood streets, slowing down just enough to safely make the sharp turns of the winding road. The engine continued to rumble as if losing breath, and for a moment Ted feared the truck would break down in the middle of the street. He kept an eye on the rearview mirror as he navigated the maze of darkened streets. The teenagers watched curiously as the truck passed by a second time, and after a few more twists and turns, Ted found the exit that would lead them home.

The two friends were silent for the rest of the drive. Frank's neighborhood was quiet as Ted pulled up in front of the cracked driveway, his friend's wife not bothering to leave the front porch light on for her husband.

"Thanks for the ride," Frank said. "And the cigar."

"No problem," Ted said.

Frank opened the passenger door and climbed out, giving Ted a two-finger salute before closing the door behind him. Ted made sure he made it inside the house before driving away.

The radio kept Ted company on his short drive home. Bright lights burned through the closed kitchen curtains. Sophie spent most nights reading paperback romances and drinking coffee, and he felt happy she was there waiting. He pulled up in the driveway, parked, killed the engine, and stepped out into the din of cicadas singing their nightly chorus.

"Hey, ice cream man!"

Ted shielded his eyes with the back of his hands to block out the sun to search for the voice in the crowd. The parade had ended several minutes ago, and after the slow-moving floats and marching bands cleared out, a swarm of people filled Main Street. As he scanned the crowd, Ted saw a tall teenager waving at him. Though he didn't recognize the boy, Ted waved back.

"My father," Emma said, by his side. "The rock star."

Ted shrugged. "What can I say?"

Having his daughter home for the holiday was special. The parade and festivities were a family tradition, and for her to take the time from her college schedule to spend time with her parents made him contented. Ted also felt a sense of relief that Emma showed up alone. Sophie revealed that their daughter's relationship with a boy at school bordered on becoming serious.

"Where we headed off to first?" Emma asked. "The music stage? The carnival?"

"I need something cool to drink first," Ted said. It wasn't even noon, and the heat was intense. The ice cream shop would've had great business, but it was an unwritten rule for the downtown stores to close to let the local charities raise money selling food and treats for the day. Besides, Ted didn't get many summer days off, especially one with Emma.

Open-air tents lined the pavement of the court-house parking lot. The first tent offered funnel cakes, and as much as it was one of Ted's favorites, he remembered his doctor's advice to eat healthier and they walked past. Another offered ice-cold root beer, but he wanted to give his money toward Sophie's fundraiser, which was at the tent at the very end.

The volunteers of St. Joseph's Catholic Church were in full action even though lunch hour was over an hour away. They didn't offer fair food or treats but rather authentic Mexican food, and Ted watched the volunteers seasoning the fajita meat and preparing the tortillas. Sophie stood at one table chopping up tomatoes, onions, and bell peppers with military precision with a kitchen knife.

"Emma?" They turned to see a young woman next to the cash register filling an empty table with napkins and plastic utensils waving toward them. "It's good to see you!"

Emma rushed over and gave the woman a hug. "You too, Diane! Can we get two sodas? Pop's buying."

"Sure thing," Diane said. She opened the ice cooler and took out two plastic bottles, wiping them off with a towel and setting them on the table.

Ted handed her a ten-dollar bill. "Keep the change."

"Thanks, Mr. Stroud. You guys coming back for lunch?"

"You know it," Emma said, holding the cold bottle against her warm cheek. "You think I'd drive into town just to hang out with my old man?"

"Funny," Ted said with a grin.

Emma leaned into Diane and whispered loud enough for Ted to hear. "I wasn't joking."

Ted twisted the cap off and took a big swig of refreshing cold soda. "Why does summer have to be so hot?"

"If you guys really want to cool off," Diane said, "you should try some gelato."

A couple of weeks had passed since Ted's nighttime incident with the food truck and the mention of gelato sent a shiver of guilt through him. He feared Brad would pay the shop a visit and demand an explanation and Ted would have to admit his embarrassing story, but the day never came.

"Great idea!" Emma said and gave Ted a mischievous grin. Sophie had filled her in on the competition while she was at school.

"There's my girl!" a voice called out from behind the smoking grill. An elderly lady with surprising agility weaved her way past the others and rushed over to Emma, giving her a big hug.

"So good to see you, Mrs. Flores." Emma returned the embrace with a big smile.

Mrs. Flores stepped away and looked at Emma from her toes to her eyes. "College's certainly agreeing with you. I bet you drive all the boys crazy."

"Maybe a few," Emma said with a knowing wink.

Mrs. Flores turned to Ted and put a warm hand on his shoulder. "Sophie! Your boyfriend's here!"

Sophie looked up from the table, knife in hand, and sighed with mock disappointment. "That's not my boyfriend, that's just my husband." She wiped the blade clean with a towel and laid it down on a clean plate before walking over. "How was the parade?

"The marching band played the same tunes as last year," Emma said. "But the cheerleaders seemed more energetic than usual."

The three women talked among themselves, and Ted listened with a courteous smile. After catching Emma up on the local gossip, Mrs. Flores excused herself, and Sophie waited until she was back behind the grill to speak.

"Have you seen the food truck?" Sophie whispered.

"Not yet," Emma said. "But Diane told us about it."

"I thought the rule was only charity fundraisers could be vendors?" Ted said.

"Ah, but you see, your friend Brad is very sneaky," Sophie said. "They're giving away free samples while taking donations for the animal shelter. A good way to promote their business."

Ted took another sip of his soda. He had to admit that Brad's strategy was a wise move for a new business in town. Almost the entire community took part in the downtown festivities, and giving away gelato would be the best advertising they could hope for.

"You both should check it out and let me know what you think. I'll be here working until after the lunch crowd dies down."

"Sure," Ted said.

"And don't tire yourselves out. I want to see some of the sights after this is over."

"We won't," Emma said. "And we'll bring you back some."

"It will only melt before you make it back. Just let me know if it's any good." Sophie walked back to the table, picked up the knife, and waved it at both. "You two have fun."

They said their goodbyes to the others and joined the crowd walking down the street. Children shouted in a joyful chorus as they jumped in the inflatable bouncy houses set up on the courthouse lawn. At the intersection of Main and Eighth, people took seats on the temporary metal bleachers set up in front of a stage where a mariachi band prepared for their performance. A section of the street was blocked off for the dancing that would begin as soon as the music started, the traffic light swaying gently above.

Behind the courthouse itself, the psychedelic colors of the *Lovely Rita* shimmered in the bright morning light. Classic sixties rock played soft enough not to interfere with the music from the stage, and a respectable line waited for their turn. Ted and Emma took their spot at the end.

"Food trucks in Howell?" Emma said. "Who would've thought. Before long, everyone will be eating organic and practicing yoga."

"As long as I don't have to grow a beard," Ted said.

"Don't worry, Pops. You're too old to be a hipster."

"You know how to hurt a guy!" Ted said, feigning dismay.

They looked over the flavors on the chalkboard menu on the side of the truck, the prices erased. The line moved steadily, and as they drew closer to the ordering window, Ted saw a small plastic barrel with a hand-drawn picture of a playful cat and dog along with the name of the animal shelter. The barrel was stuffed with bills, and Ted took a few from his wallet and added them to the total.

"What are you going to get?" Emma asked.

"Strawberry, I think."

"Boring!" Emma said with a laugh. "Look at all those flavors. Be bold!"

A young red-haired woman greeted them from the other side of the window when they reached the front. Not much older than Emma, she offered them both a wide smile.

"Welcome! How can I help you?"

"Can you tell me about the stracciatella?" Emma said.

"Sure, it's rich and creamy vanilla gelato with very thin shreds of chocolate. Very traditional, and very good. It's probably my favorite."

"Sounds great, I'll have that."

"And for you, sir?"

"I'll try apple pie," Ted said.

Emma smiled. "Way to go, Dad. Live a little bit."

"Perfect for the Fourth," the woman said, writing both down and passing the note along. "No charge today, and thanks for the donation!"

They waited by the window, the music of the mariachi band from the stage setting a festive mood. Someone pushed two paper cups with gelato out the window and Ted reached out for them.

"Mr. Stroud!" Brad said. "Rita, this is the ice cream shop owner I was telling you about."

The young woman's eyes lit up. "Oh, hi! Brad told me all about your shop. I've been meaning to stop by, but we've been busy."

"Understandable," Ted said. "This is my daughter, Emma. She's visiting from college."

"Nice to meet both of you," Rita said. She stuck her arm out the window and shook both of their hands. "What are you studying, Emma?"

"It's my first year, so just the basics. Math's not my strong suit, so I'm taking algebra this summer so I can have only one class to focus on."

"Once upon a time, I studied psychology," Rita said. "Before I let this guy talk me into this business.

Good luck with your class."

"Thanks, I'll need it," Emma said. "Nice meeting both of you."

"Maybe next time you're in town, we can go out for coffee."

Emma's face lit up. "That'd be nice."

Ted picked up their cups as Rita and Brad waved goodbye. Emma hustled over to an empty picnic table under the shade of an oak tree on the courtyard lawn and claimed it before anyone else could. Ted placed the cups down and took a seat across from her as the festive music of the mariachi band swept over the downtown street. He took a spoonful of his gelato, studying the smooth and creamy texture as a gentle breeze rustled through the leaves above them. He brought the spoon to his open mouth.

"What do you think?" Emma asked.

"Different, like ice cream with a little more spice. Lots of flavor."

Emma smiled, taking a taste of her own. "That's good. Here, have some of mine."

They exchanged paper cups across the table, dipping in their spoons and taking a hefty amount of each other's gelato and trying them at the same time.

"That's almost as good as real apple pie," Emma said.

"I think I like yours better," Ted said. "What's it called again?"

"Stracciatella. It's the chocolate flakes that makes

it."

Other families gathered around them, either at other tables or lying on blankets spread out on the lush, green grass. A group of laughing small children ran around them, reminding Ted of Emma at the same age. He remembered the time she lost her balloon, a sudden gust of wind whisking it out of her hand and into the deep blue sky. She was on the verge of tears, Sophie comforting her as Ted rushed back to the balloon vendor. He hurried back and showed Emma the balloon as Sophie tied the string gently around her wrist and he watched as sadness gave way to joy.

"Earth to Dad."

Ted blinked his eyes, the memory slipping away. "Yes?"

"I asked if you wanted to head back. It's getting close to noon."

"Sure," Ted said. "Time's flown by today."

Ted stood, took both of their cups, and tossed them in the trash can by the oak tree. Emma joined his side as their table was quickly taken by a large family who couldn't believe their luck. They walked away from the courthouse and back onto the street, the music fading away. The collective aroma from the food tents beckoned them, and by the time they reached the church tent, the line stretched along the street like a snake. They had taken their place at the end when Sophie walked up to them carrying three paper plates wrapped in foil.

"They have plenty of help now, so I got off early," Sophie said as she handed them their plates. "After we eat and look around a bit, I'll come back to help clean up."

"Sounds good to me," Emma said. "I'm starving."

As a family they weaved their way through the crowd. Up ahead, the doors of the community theater building were propped open and, seeking refuge from the heat, they stepped inside. Most of the seats were empty but the stage was filled with parents, teachers, and students rehearsing for the annual Fourth of July program scheduled for that evening. They took a seat in the back row and quietly took the foil off their plates to not disturb the proceedings.

With a mammoth American flag hanging behind them, a group of high school students sang "Yankee Doodle Dandy" as Mr. Ratcliff, the longtime theater arts teacher, watched from the side of the stage. The Fourth of July program was a rite of passage for young people with dreams of fame, and even though it was merely a rehearsal, they sang with all their might. When the song ended, Emma and Sophie set their plates on their laps and clapped. Mr. Ratcliff searched the auditorium through his thick glasses as the choir gave an awkward collective bow, not realizing they had been performing for an audience.

Like the most memorable summer days, the rest of the afternoon passed by in a carefree blur. Emma bought a baseball cap to support the town's Little League, and Sophie bought a pair of cheap sunglasses. They watched the annual pie-eating contest and weren't surprised that the thin fireman with a bushy moustache who won every year was victorious again.

As evening approached, they headed over to the courthouse for a family photo. The gazebo was adorned with red, white, and blue bunting, and a kind man offered to take their picture with Emma's phone. Ted put one arm around Sophie and the other around his daughter, all smiling wide for the camera. The man cheerfully took several photos before handing the phone back to Emma.

"Beautiful family you got there," the man said to Ted.

"Thank you," Ted beamed proudly.

Emma and Ted led Sophie over to the *Lovely Rita*, but as they drew closer, they saw no one standing in line and the ordering window closed. A piece of paper was taped over the menu with the words *Sold out! Thank you everyone for your donations!*

"That's alright," Sophie said. "Summer just started; I'll have plenty of other chances to try some."

They returned to the church tent to help clean up. Most of the other vendors had already packed up, leaving empty tents, and a small group of volunteers walked along Main Street picking up scattered trash. The local brass band unloaded their instruments at the courthouse gazebo, preparing to take the stage to perform accompaniment to the night's fireworks show. Some families had already spread their blankets on the ground to get the best view.

The volunteers folded and packed the plastic tables in the back of the church bus, and Ted helped the other husbands and boyfriends load the mammoth smoker on the back of the priest's truck. They said their goodbyes and stood on the sidewalk as the vehicles drove off. As children scampered on the playground and adults played softball at the Little League park, they walked toward the neon sign of Stroud's Ice Cream Shop.

Ted reached into his pocket, found his keys, and opened the store door. They were greeted with a wave of air-conditioned air as he stepped inside and turned on the lights, the shopkeeper's bell welcoming them with a metallic clang.

"I swear, every year it gets hotter and hotter," Sophie said. She walked to the refrigerator and grabbed a handful of ice cubes, dropping them into a glass. The ice crackled as she put the glass under the faucet and turned on the water.

Emma took down a chair from the top of a table and sat down. "Makes you think climate change might be a real thing."

"It's summer," Ted said as he walked over to the cash register. The concept of climate change was one of the few things Ted and Emma argued about. "It's supposed to be hot."

"No politics," Sophie said, holding the cold glass to her forehead. "It's the Fourth of July. Let's pretend everything is just peachy with the country."

Ted smiled as he opened the cash register. He scooped up a handful of quarters and walked over to the jukebox and plugged in the cord. The neon colors flashed to life and Ted fed a quarter into the slot, picking out a handful of his favorite '50s songs. He stepped back as the wail of Little Richard singing "Rip It Up" filled the dining room.

"Hey, beautiful," Ted said as he playfully bobbed to Sophie's side. "Want to dance?"

Sophie took a big gulp of her ice water before setting the glass down on the counter. "How can I refuse such a handsome man?"

Ted took her hand and led her to the middle of the room. Emma looked up from her phone and watched them with a smile. At first, their dance moves were stiff and shaky, but soon both were swaying their hips and clapping their hands with the beat.

"You two are embarrassing your poor daughter," Emma said as she covered her eyes.

"Stop being a hater and join us," Sophie said, extending her hand.

Emma shook her head. "I'll leave the dancing to the professionals."

Sophie shrugged and spun back to Ted, the bright

lights of the jukebox sparkling in her eyes. The next song was a Jerry Lee Lewis rocker, and as that song wound down, Ted needed to catch his breath. As the mechanical arm lifted the next record onto the turntable, Ted put his hands on his knees.

"Come on, old man," Sophie said playfully. She put a supporting hand on his shoulder. "Have another song in you?"

"Only if it's a slow one."

As if the jukebox read his mind, the haunting harmonies of the Flamingos' *I Only Have Eyes for You* filled the room like thin smoke. A wide smile crept over Ted's face as he formally offered his hand. "May I have this dance?"

"Why, I'd be honored, Mr. Stroud," Sophie said with an exaggerated Southern accent, and then she took his hand. Ted gently pulled her toward him and placed an arm around her waist. Together they shuffled under the harsh store light, careful not to bump into the tables. As they swayed back and forth, Ted looked deeply into Sophie's eyes. The moment would become a treasured memory.

The sun set and the stars twinkled in the dark clear sky outside the shop windows. Each of the three filled a big plastic bowl with several scoops of their favorite flavors of ice cream and stepped into the alley behind the shop, climbing the metal fire escape steps that led to the roof of the building. Ted always kept several lawn chairs at the ready, and the roof gave them a great view of the courthouse lawn and the horizon beyond.

On the gazebo stage three little girls, each dressed in red, white, and blue dance outfits, sang the national anthem with all their hearts. The crowd applauded, and the girls took the acclamation in with wide smiles as the mayor, Marc Parker, climbed the steps to deliver his welcoming remarks.

Like most of his friends, Ted had known Marc Parker since elementary school. Marc's father had been bank president, and Marc followed in his footsteps. The mayor loved the sound of his voice almost as much as he loved money, and Ted's thoughts wandered about halfway through his speech. Finally, the mayor finished and the opening chords of *Stars and Stripes Forever* filled the downtown streets.

Out of the corner of his eye, Ted saw a large shadow move across the parking lot behind the courthouse. The rumbling music drowned out the festive music for a few moments as the *Lovely Rita* crept out of the parking lot and onto the backstreet. He watched the truck's red taillights head off into the distance as the first fireworks exploded across the night sky.

Dust drifted toward the floor, twinkling in the bright morning light, as Ted stood on a ladder and swept the ceiling fans with a washcloth. The amount of dirt that could collect in a few days always amazed him, and the chore seemed nothing short of futile. Sophie had left to make her pilgrimage to the bank for a fresh supply of cash and coins for the register. In the past, she needed to make the trip at least once a day, but now with most customers using credit cards, it was a weekly task. On Saturday, the bank stayed open until noon, and Sophie preferred to conduct her business with the small weekend crowds over the busy weekdays.

Across the street, Ted watched the morning walkers and joggers at the park from the open window blinds. The bright morning sun promised nothing but stifling heat, and everyone wanted to get their workouts in early. He stepped off the ladder and moved it to the next fan when a shadow passed across the walls of the shop. Across the park, Ted saw the *Lovely Rita* pull up into the baseball field parking lot.

The shopkeeper's bell clanged as Sophie entered, clutching her purse to her chest. She gave Ted a smile as she walked over to the cash register, punched in the security code, and placed the bills and coins in their respective slots when the till opened.

"What are you staring at?" she asked. "Is there a cute college girl jogging around the track?"

"Come here for a moment," Ted said, not taking his gaze away from the parking lot.

Sophie shut the register and walked over, shielding her eyes with her hand as Ted pointed out the window.

"What am I supposed to be seeing?"

"Might need your glasses?" Ted said.

Sophie muttered in Spanish and took out her bifocals from her blouse pocket. Almost half-blind without them, she was too vain to wear them unless necessary. She slipped them on, blinked her eyes to focus, and turned back to the window.

"Bastard," she whispered, her eyes wide.

"Come on, you can do better than that! Throw in some of those dirty Spanish words you're so fond of. Let them have it!"

Sophie crossed her arms over her chest. They watched through the blinds as Brad stepped out of the truck, followed by Rita, skipping like a teenager to the front of the truck. She struck a pose as Brad snapped a photo with his phone, and suddenly Ted was reminded of Emma and how she archived her entire high school years on social media with an avalanche of daily photos.

"I'll be right back," Ted said and walked toward his office. "I need to look something up on the computer."

"I thought I'd never hear those words coming out of your mouth," Sophie said. "Let me know if I you need any help."

"Very funny," Ted said from the hallway. He

opened the door and stepped inside.

The desktop computer was old and bulky, sitting on the heavily scratched wood desk Ted had purchased at a garage sale years ago. The screen blazed to life when he pushed the power button, a pop-up asking for his user ID and password.

"Sophie," he called out, but she was already standing at the open doorway. She walked over, typed in a series of letters and numbers on the keyboard, and stepped away.

"Thanks," Ted said.

"*De nada.*"

Ted pulled his chair up to the desk and watched the display icons load up on the screen. The office was mainly Sophie's domain, where she made orders and kept up with business records, and Ted always felt uncomfortable using the computer. Afraid he'd delete a vital piece of information with a wrong click of the mouse, Ted carefully moved the cursor to the internet icon and clicked it.

Emma had shown him how to use the search engine and Ted typed in the words *Lovely Rita*, *gelato*, *truck*, and *Howell Texas*. The first results that popped up referred to the Beatles, but after Ted had scrolled through a few, Brad's business link appeared.

Ted clicked on the link and the food truck instantly filled the screen. Below the photo of the food truck was a business description along with brief bios of both Brad and Rita. Ted moved the cursor to the righthand corner and hovered over the menu where the *Events* option popped up. He clicked on it and instantly the photo he witnessed being taken appeared onscreen.

A smiling Rita posed in front of the truck in the Little League parking lot, the scoreboard and American flag in the background. Ted was amazed how fast today's world moved, that a photo taken several minutes before could appear on his computer in a matter of minutes.

"No respect," Sophie muttered as she joined Ted's side.

"I don't understand," Ted said. "The concession stands need to make money, so I'm sure the Little League officials will ask them to leave. They probably didn't know better. Besides, with the playoffs and all, they'll need all the parking spaces they can get."

"I wouldn't count on it," Sophie said, shaking her head.

"We'll wait and see," Ted said. Hopefully the problem would resolve itself.

"I think that time has passed," Sophie said as she walked back to the doorway. "We have to start standing up for ourselves."

"How? You want me to walk over there and tell them to move?"

"That's exactly what I want you to do. Also tell them to never park downtown ever again. They're taking away our business." She rapped her knuckles on the door for emphasis before walking back to the dining room.

Ted sat back and rubbed his eyes. A confrontation was the last thing he wanted, but deep down a quiet fury stirred. Stroud's Ice Cream Shop had been a mainstay of the town for generations, but the *Lovely Rita* served as a direct attack on the family's legacy. It also served as a reminder of how things could change at the drop of a hat.

From the dining room, Ted heard Sophie greeting a customer. He logged off the computer and pushed himself away from the desk. His bones creaked as he stood up and let out a deep sigh at the long day of work ahead.

It turned out to be one of their busiest days of the summer. A steady stream of customers kept Ted's mind so occupied that he'd almost forgotten about the rival truck. The morning hours passed quickly and before he knew it, it was time to prepare for the scheduled afternoon birthday party. Sophie watched over the dining room as Ted shut the office door and changed into his festive clown suit, which became tighter every time he put it on.

Ted walked over to the filing cabinet and took out the box of makeup he used for his transformation. It took only a few minutes to apply the basic but traditional clown face, and when he was done, he studied his reflection as he straightened his jumbo bow tie. Through the closed office door, he could hear the voices of the guests and waited for Sophie to give him his cue.

A couple of minutes later, Sophie knocked. "Showtime!"

He opened the office door, walked softly down the hallway, and stepped into the dining room with a huge smile on his face and arms extended. The group of children shouted with surprise and joy as Ted greeted each one of them with a handshake or a bump of the fist. When he reached the boy with a paper crown on his head, Ted put a hand on his shoulder.

"You must be the birthday boy!"

The boy nodded.

"Well, happy birthday! How about all of us play some games, what do you say?"

The boy and the rest of the children cheered.

The party games went on without a hitch. A shy girl won pin the tail on the donkey, instantly bolstering her confidence. Ted made each child a balloon animal, the squeaking rubber and his dramatic twisting and tying entertaining the group as Sophie broke away to retrieve the birthday cake. Though he never mastered the technique of his father, his balloon animals were passable. He gave the best one to the birthday boy, telling him it was a dinosaur that was originally supposed to be a giraffe.

Sophie asked the children to sit down at the table. Parents gave Ted smiles of approval as he made his way around the room closing the window blinds. The children grew quiet with anticipation as Ted stood at the switch, checking to see if Sophie was ready, and turned the lights off. Sophie lifted the cake from behind the counter, the candles giving light to the room, as Ted motioned like a symphony conductor for everyone to sing.

"Happy Birthday…" Ted began, his singing soon drowned out by the children and parents joining in. Sophie walked slowly to the table and set the cake down in front of the birthday boy. The candles lit up his happy face as the song ended with a flourish.

"Kids," Ted called out. "What does the birthday boy do now?"

"Make a wish!" several children shouted.

"Close his eyes!" a couple of others yelled.

Scratching his head, Ted gave a comedic confused look with his clown face. "So, you make a wish, then close your eyes?"

"No!" the children yelled in unison.

"Okay, then you blow out the candles, close your eyes, and make a wish?"

"No!" the group shouted even louder.

Ted feigned a look of intense concentration before breaking out with a smile. "Wait, I think I got it! You close your eyes, make a wish, then blow out the candles?"

"Yes!"

The clown nodded. "And what happens after

that?"

"We eat cake!" the children shouted, joined in by a few of the parents. Ted playfully stumbled backwards, as if the force of their voices was strong enough to push him.

"Oh, right! That's my favorite part!"

Sophie cut the first and largest slice for the birthday boy and slid it to her husband on a plastic plate. Ted picked it up and placed it on the table before the wide-eyed boy. Sophie possessed an innate talent for cutting just the right number of slices for all the kids and parents and, within minutes, Ted had handed everyone their piece of cake.

Birthday parties always were a vital part of the Strouds' business. For a reasonable fee, they took the stress and worry away from the parents by handling everything from the decorations and party games to the birthday cake itself. Sophie baked and decorated the cakes and took pride in the positive reaction they always received.

Although Ted's father had purchased the clown costume many years ago, the colors were still vibrant. Sophie had only needed to make a few repairs every now and then, which were easily done with needle and thread. The kids loved it, and other than being hot and uncomfortable, Ted always enjoyed creating another childhood memory.

After the guests finished their cake, Ted would dramatically sweep the dirty plates and plastic forks into the trash bag Sophie held open. In no time the tables were cleared and Ted brought the first present over from gifts stacked next to the jukebox.

"Be sure to read the card first," Ted whispered to the birthday boy. The boy nodded and read the card in a dull voice before handing it back to Ted. He ripped through the wrapping to reveal a basketball small enough for his tiny hands.

"Thank you," the boy muttered, setting it aside and waiting for the next one.

The parade of presents continued for several minutes, some appreciated more than others. Finally, Ted handed over the final wrapped box from the boy's parents. Not unusually large or heavy, Ted wondered what it would be. The boy's eyes grew wide as shredded wrapping paper fell to the floor.

Like a balloon pop, the boy's cheerful shout filled the room as he held up a box over his head in victory. It was a video game console and, judging by the excitement the box generated, a popular one. Several kids jumped out of their chairs, almost as if they couldn't believe in such a miracle, and the boy's parents smiled with satisfaction.

Sophie grabbed the camera from behind the counter and asked the birthday boy, his parents, and the clown to gather for a photo. With all the cell phones present among the party guests, there would be hundreds of photos to document the occasion, but this would be the one that would be placed on the wall of the shop. For a few seconds they stood still and smiled until Sophie got the shot.

And in what seemed like a flash, the party was over. The guests made their way to the door as the birthday boy and his mother handed each child a small bag of toys and candy in appreciation for coming. The father and several other parents made a couple of trips to take the presents to the family car as the dining room emptied.

"Did you have a good time?" Ted the clown asked the boy.

"Yes, I did," the boy said shyly.

"What was your favorite part?"

The boy didn't hesitate with his answer. "The video game! I can't wait to get home to play it!"

The mother smiled as she shook both Ted's and Sophie's hands, thanking them for hosting a great party. The father stepped back in, wiping sweat from his brow, and discreetly handed Ted a twenty-dollar tip. Sophie asked them to wait for a moment, went to the office, and came back with a freshly printed photo of the family and the clown in front of the jukebox. The parents thanked them again before they stepped out into the bright sunlight.

The sudden silence of the dining room unsettled Ted. He picked up the trash bags full of paper plates and wrapping paper and headed toward the door. "I think that went pretty well."

"You should stay in your costume all day," Sophie

said. "Business might pick up if word got around."

"Too hot of a day for that," Ted said.

With a trash bag in each hand, he stepped outside and walked past the antique store next door toward the alley dumpster. Several folks at the park across the street gave him a strange look as he lifted the lid and threw the bags in. A thunderous cheer erupted from the Little League stands, and when he looked toward the scoreboard to see which team was winning, Ted saw a long line of people winding through the parking lot. With all the birthday party preparation, the *Lovely Rita* had left his thoughts until now.

Pure rage suddenly surged through him. Ted walked across the street, not bothering to check for oncoming traffic. The children's playful laughter turned to silence as he walked by the playground. The clown makeup slowly melted in the heat with black and red droplets dripping on the pom-pom buttons of his costume. Ted knew he must look like a monster from childhood nightmares and turned away from the playground, cutting across the walking trail and heading straight for the gelato truck.

The dead, dusty brown grass crunched under his feet as he reached the curb of the parking lot. Another cheer erupted at the crack of the bat as the people in line noticed the melting clown. He stopped for a moment to control his anger, thinking of the best approach, when a deep, authoritative voice called out to him.

"What are you doing, out here like this?"

Ted shielded his eyes from the sunlight as a tall, shadowy figure approached. Wearing black shorts, gray t-shirt, and the baseball cap of his son's baseball team, he recognized the man as Marc Parker. The casual look of the mayor and bank manager, usually dressed in a conservative suit and ties, unsettled him.

Ted tilted his head toward the truck. "I need to talk with the owner."

Marc's eyes darted around, aware of the crowd in line a few feet away. "Calm down, Ted. I've never seen you like this before."

Ted glanced down at his costume. "We had a birthday at the shop."

"That's not what I meant."

Marc took Ted by his arm and led him back to the grass. "You're stomping around like you want to punch someone in the face."

Ted kept his eyes on the truck. "You're right about that. They're taking my business away."

A mother put a protective arm around her young daughter as they walked by. Hoping to diffuse their concern, Marc gave them a comforting smile.

"Listen," Marc whispered, turning back to Ted. "I understand your situation."

"You do? Then why are you allowing them to sell their stuff in the Little League parking lot? Who would walk a hundred yards in this heat to my shop when they can just grab one here?"

"It wasn't my decision."

"I'm sure the mayor has enough political sway with the almighty Little League commissioner."

"Look, this is just a fad. Folks will try it for a few weeks, get tired of it, then head right back to your shop. People like all the new, glittery stuff until it's not new and glittery anymore."

Marc put a hand on Ted's shoulder, guiding him to look across the park toward his shop. The Stroud Ice Cream shop sign stood out from the cornerstone of Main Street like a beacon, having stood for over forty years. So many other downtown stores had come and gone, but Stroud's remained.

"I've been meaning to stop by, but this summer's been crazy," Marc said as they walked toward the street. "But I will stop by soon. I may have some good news for you."

"Good news?"

"Yes, but I can't really talk about it now. Nothing's confirmed, don't want to give you false hope. And this is just between us, so please don't share with anyone."

"Even Sophie?"

Marc grinned. "No offense, but Sophie knows everyone in this town. Let's keep it on the hush-hush for now."

Ted considered the possibilities for a few moments before nodding his head.

"When I have more details, I'll stop by and discuss with both of you. But right now, I'd like for you to go back inside and take off that clown makeup and costume. You look like a serial killer out here."

Marc gave Ted a reassuring pat on the shoulder and headed back toward the baseball field. Ted's senses, dulled by anger, now came back as his feet burned and blistered in the cheap plastic clown shoes. He whisked the footwear off and walked back across the street in his socks.

"How did it go?" Sophie asked when he stepped back inside.

Ted took the crumpled twenty-dollar bill from his costume pocket and handed it to her.

"What's this for?"

"For being right," Ted said, pointing toward the window.

Sophie walked over and peeked through the blinds. Ted walked down the hallway as his wife unleashed a string of obscenities in Spanish that would make her church congregation blush. He stepped into the bathroom, turned on the water, and splashed warm water on his face as the vivid colors of the clown makeup swirled down the drain.

God, how he loved that woman.

"And can I also get a shot of bourbon?" Ted asked.

The waitress looked surprised as she sat a new pitcher of beer on the table.

"Slow down, partner," Frank said.

"Don't worry about me," Ted said with a grin and nodded to the waitress, who whisked the empty pitcher off the table and headed back to the bar.

August had brought stormy weather that put Ted in a deep funk. Labor Day loomed on the horizon and his business had been on a steady downward spiral. Summer was about to be over, school would start soon, and Sophie's time and focus would be back to her teaching duties, having little time for anything else. With Emma away, the thought of lonely days filled him with dread.

The bar was different this time of night. Ted and Frank typically left before the band finished their set, but tonight they watched their last song before the musicians broke down their equipment and carried their instruments out the door. Most of the other patrons sat alone, either with their heads down staring at their drinks or watching sports highlights with vacant eyes. The bartender seemed immune to it all as he washed and rinsed glasses and then set them on the rack to dry.

"You don't usually touch the hard stuff," Frank said after the waitress returned with a full shot glass. "Is there something you want to talk about?"

"Nothing really," Ted said as he picked up the glass and studied it. "Just a little fight with the missus."

"We've all been there, my friend."

Ted brought the glass to his lips and quickly tilted it back. The bourbon screeched down his throat as he set the shot glass down on the table. "Sophie's always been the brains of the operation."

Frank feigned shock. "You don't say!"

"She looked over the books and it's all bad news. Not that I didn't suspect as much, but to see it laid out in black and white was disheartening, to say the least. We barely covered expenses, and with Emma's tuition and all, I don't know how much longer we can keep going."

He waited for his best friend to reassure him that everything would work out, but Frank only nodded his head in sympathy.

"Sophie wants me to be more aggressive," Ted continued. "Promoting, advertising, all that stuff I hate. Hell, we've been in the same spot for forty years. Everyone in town knows where we're at; I don't need to waste money to remind them."

"I think she has a point," Frank said. "People are moving in all the time, and a lot of those folks don't know our businesses even exist. A little promotion might get your face out there."

Ted tapped the empty shot glass several times on the table, thinking it over, but he couldn't let Frank know it wasn't only financial woes that worried him. He wasn't sure if he could even put the sensation in words, only the realization that the shop's time had passed.

"Did you hear about the festival they're having at the fairgrounds on Labor Day weekend?" Ted asked.

"I have," Frank said as he refilled both glasses with beer.

"They're going to have all kinds of music and lots of food. The good stuff: corn dogs, funnel cakes, gelato."

Frank ran his finger around the rim of his mug. "See, that's your problem right there. You let this guy make you so upset. But if you think about it, with summer almost over, this is probably his last hurrah until next year."

"I don't know which I feel worse about," Ted said. "This festival or summer's winding down. I wonder how many we have left?"

Frank gave Ted a stunned look. "You're just a barrel of laughs tonight."

The waitress came by and picked up the empty shot glass. "Another?" she asked with a bored smile.

Ted shrugged his shoulders. "Why not?"

"Listen," Fred began. "When the megastore opened down the road, I didn't see how we could survive. But I went in there out of curiosity, seeing how the enemy operates, and you know what?"

"What?"

"Not one employee said a word to me. They couldn't care less if I bought something or not.

Hourly employees, so what do they care if you buy a hammer? And you know what?"

Ted shook his head.

"My business started to pick up. Maybe not in great numbers, but I started seeing new faces along with the regulars. And I realized most folks are like me. They don't just want to buy a hammer; they want to talk to someone about why they want to buy a hammer. People crave that few minutes of human interaction."

The waitress returned and handed Ted the new shot glass full of whiskey. He held it out toward Frank. "My friend, the philosopher."

Frank smiled and picked up his glass of beer. "Here's to two old farts trying to make sense of this strange world."

They clinked their glasses in a toast.

Not much of a hard drinker, Ted hesitantly brought the shot glass to his lips. A couple of pitchers of beer among friends were as far as he would usually allow himself to go, but the first shot of hard liquor seemed to have little effect. Ted tilted the glass back and felt the alcohol burn down his throat again, but this time it struck him like a kick in the gut from a mule, as if the alcohol was waiting to wreak havoc in his bloodstream.

"Be right back," Ted said. Slightly dizzy, he grabbed the back of his chair to stand.

Ted followed the lights of the jukebox toward

the restrooms. He knew the path by heart, but his feet felt heavy and dull. The bartender gave him a concerned look as he passed by.

"Feeling okay, chief?" the bartender asked.

"Fine," Ted said with a wave of his hands. The bartender nodded but didn't seem convinced.

He pushed the restroom door open as the harsh light pierced his eyes followed by the putrid smell that caused his stomach to churn. The old saying *beer before liquor, never sicker* popped in his head, and he regretted he hadn't remembered it sooner. There was only one stall, and Ted gave silent thanks that it was unoccupied. He kneeled on the floor, lifted the lid, and heaved his bar tab into the rusty bowl.

After regaining his composure, Ted looked up at a flyer posted on the wall among the crude drawings and scrawled graffiti. Arms crossed and wearing proud smiles, Brad and Rita stood in front of the *Lovely Rita* as if nothing but good fortune lay in their future. Looking at Brad's thick beard and self-satisfied superiority, Ted had the sudden urge to slap the smug smile off his face.

With one grand swoop he ripped the poster off the wall and shredded it into pieces. The destruction felt satisfying, and as he stepped out of the stall, he threw the pieces into the air like confetti.

The restroom door opened, and an older man looked at Ted with concern as the shreds of paper fell to the floor.

"All yours," Ted said as he walked past him and out the door.

The walk back to the table seemed to take twice as long as the one to the toilet, and when Ted sat back down, he let out a long exhale. The room spun slightly, and he realized he might have had one drink too many. He rubbed his eyes, and when he opened them the colors and light of the room were almost blinding.

"You okay, friend?" Frank asked. "You don't look so good."

"I'm all right," Ted said, trying to shake it off. "Just need to lay off the hard stuff."

Frank watched Ted pour himself another glass. "You have to promise me that you'll let me drive home tonight."

Ted raised his glass and took a sip of the cold, tasty beer. "I can always count on you, Frank."

An older couple lay down their cue sticks at the pool table as a maudlin country song started on the jukebox. Ted watched with fascination as the couple two-stepped across the floor in perfect harmony, their boots scraping wood with every step. When the song ended, the man dipped his partner until her long hair touched the floor, and when he lifted her back up, he gave her a passionate kiss.

Though still relatively early in the evening, the dancing couple would be the last image Ted would remember from the night.

The closed window blinds were little help in blocking out the early morning sun. Tiny dust particles danced in the light as Ted sat at his desk, face in his hands, with the hope that two aspirins and a refreshing glass of ice-cold water would be the remedy for his pulsing headache. Though they needed business, a small part of him hoped the day would be very slow. The thought of engaging with customers seemed a monumental task in his current state.

The office door was open, and down the hallway Ted saw Sophie sitting alone in the dining room. He envied her simple ritual of waiting for the workday to begin by reading her current paperback while enjoying her cup of coffee. Most days, catching her in these quiet moments would bring him joy, but today it made him feel foolish and jealous.

On the computer screen, a childhood photo of Emma smiling with her hands on her hips greeted him. The image was bittersweet, causing him to mourn the speed of time but also instilling contentment that they had raised a girl who had become a confident young adult ready to take on the world. He moved the computer mouse until the arrow lined up with the email icon and clicked it.

The unopened emails loaded onscreen, mainly advertisements from pharmaceutical companies or offers of student financial aid, two subjects he'd recently researched. He deleted them until an email from Emma popped up. Ted immediately clicked it open.

Hope you don't mind, but I created a social media page for the shop!

Below her message, a link was highlighted in blue. Ted clicked on it and another screen popped up showing a young Ted and Sophie standing proudly in front of the shop. Instantly he remembered the blustery fall day the photo was taken, only a month or so after his father's passing, but the image betrayed not sorrow but the hope of a young couple with their entire lives ahead of them.

Toward the bottom of the page, the shop location and hours were listed along with glowing comments that seemed to be from loyal customers but were probably from Emma herself:

Been a loyal customer since I was a kid! Best ice cream in town!

You won't find better people than the Strouds!

Had a great birthday party for our son. Sophie created such a wonderful cake, and Ted is the perfect clown!

Ted moved the cursor over the word *Photos* and saw a black-and-white photo of his father, not a day over thirty, watching his young son happily eating a bowl of ice cream at the shop. The same jukebox that currently sat in the dining room was pictured just over his left shoulder. He clicked the mouse and another memory appeared, this one of his mother celebrating her birthday with all of her family and friends surrounding her. He clicked again and this time brought up a photo of a younger Sophie hugging a five-year-old Emma under the Strouds' sign on a bright sunny day.

But it was the last photo that touched Ted the deepest. Dressed in his clown suit and makeup, Ted's father was holding a baby Emma in his lap at her first birthday party. The photo was taken a few years after his father's retirement, and it would be the last photo of them together before his health took a turn for the worse. His father would pass away only a few months later.

Like having a magic trick explained to you and realizing how simple it truly is, Ted now saw the power of social media. He spent a few minutes reading the history of the shop that Emma had written, then scrolled through the dozen or so names that had "liked" the page, old friends appearing out of the blue. He clicked on some of the familiar faces, catching up on the lives that had drifted in and out of the shop for years. Before he knew it, a half hour had passed when Brad Wilkinson entered the shop and reminded Ted of his headache.

Sophie greeted the visitor as Ted walked down the hallway from his office. He looked up to see Brad standing at the counter, his heavily tattooed arms crossed against his chest and a scowl on his face. The temperature in the room instantly heated up a few degrees, it seemed, with tension in the air.

"Good morning, Brad," Ted said.

"Morning," Brad replied firmly.

"Haven't seen you in a while. How's summer treating you?"

Brad uncrossed his arms. "Not so good, now that you ask. We had a little trouble in our neighborhood last night."

"What kind of trouble?" Sophie asked.

"Someone thought it would be amusing to slash the tires on our food truck."

"That's terrible." Sophie stood up and offered Brad a seat at her table. "Sit down, I'll make you a cup of coffee."

"No, thank you," Brad said, not taking his eyes off Ted. "It's easy enough to buy new tires, but the thought of someone doing such a low-down thing is miserable. First house on the block and we already need security cameras."

Sophie shook her head with sympathy. "The world today."

"The truck alarm goes off," Brad continued. "It's sensitive, sometimes a gust of wind or a cat rubbing against it can set it off. I went to turn it off when I saw the tires."

Ted rubbed his forehead, the headache returning full force. For some inexplicable reason, a surge of guilt swept through him. The events of the early morning were foggy, and the last concrete image he could remember was the dancing couple at the bar.

Brad continued. "A group of teenagers hangs around the construction on the next block at night. They're harmless, just some smoking and drinking to pass the time. I'm an early morning person and try to get my three-mile jog in before the sun rises, and sometimes I stop by and visit. They remind me of myself at that age, no direction, letting the days slip by. I try to talk with them, see what's going on, maybe give them a little encouragement."

"That's kind of you," Sophie said, then took a sip of coffee.

"Ashamed to admit it, but when I saw my slashed tires, I thought it was them. I confronted them but they were adamant they had nothing to do with it. They did say they noticed a pickup truck driving around the neighborhood late in the night. I thought they were making up a story, but the more they talked, the more I believed them."

"What are you getting at?" Sophie asked in a firm but calm voice. "My husband drives a truck, but then again, most folks in this town drive trucks."

Brad kept his eyes on Ted. "A few weeks ago, I heard about the episode at the park. An angry clown scaring little kids straight from a Stephen King story."

Sophie stood up. "I'm sorry, but I can't allow you to disrespect my husband like this."

Brad spun and turned his angry gaze to her. "Slashing someone's tires outside of their house is disrespectful. I don't think you should be preaching to me."

Oh no, Ted thought as he closed his eyes. *There would be no turning back from Sophie's wrath now.* He opened his eyes and saw Sophie standing very still, returning Brad's gaze with one that could cut glass.

"Mr. Wilkinson, you've been disrespecting my husband ever since you arrived." Her voice was calm but with just a hint of Spanish inflection that added venom to her speech. "Parking your truck right across from our store. Taking away our business."

"Like it or not, I live here, too. I have just as much right to sell my product as you."

"Product? Call us old-fashioned, but we sell ice cream."

And then Brad made a noise one should never, ever make in Sophie's presence: a snicker. By instinct, Ted immediately rushed over and weaved himself between the two.

"If competition's too much for your quaint small-town ice cream shop," Brad said, "that's not my problem."

"Quaint?" Sophie smiled sarcastically. "If you think your food truck's hipper and more modern than our shop, more power to you."

"Look," Ted said and held up both of his hands. "This heat's got us all on edge. Brad, I understand you're upset, but I assure you I didn't slash your tires. It's your right not to believe me, but you had your say."

He walked over to the glass door, the bell clanging as he held it open. Brad took one last look around the shop, nodding to them both as he walked out, the bell repeating its clang as Ted let the door close behind him.

The sudden silence in the room made Ted tense. Sophie watched Brad walking away through the window blinds for a few moments, then turned to Ted. "I'll get us some more coffee."

"I didn't do anything," Ted said as he sat down at a table. He tried putting the pieces of last night's events in focus, but they remained dark and blurry. Sophie walked over and set the coffee cup on the table in front of him. The aroma soothed his pounding headache.

"Relax," Sophie said as she sat down across from him.

She picked up her paperback and returned to her mystery. Though Ted wanted nothing more than to lock himself up in his office and shut out the world, the quiet moment under the slight breeze of the ceiling fan relaxed him. For the first time he could remember, Ted hoped there wouldn't be any customers for the rest of the day.

Mother Nature waited until summer's end to unleash its full fury.

Early August showers released a thick humidity along with the record-breaking high temperatures that made the last few days unbearable. Though the heat brought in business, Ted secretly wished he could trade a bit of his profit for more comfortable weather.

The day before, Ted took the afternoon off to take Emma to a movie. Her summer semester had ended, and he was happy to have his daughter home for a few weeks before the fall semester began. While Sophie preferred reading, Emma had inherited her father's love of the silver screen. Sophie watched the shop, and father and daughter snuck out to see the big summer blockbuster before it left town.

The plot was silly and the special effects and theme music over the top, but Ted enjoyed leaving the real world behind for an afternoon. They stayed through the end credits, getting their money's worth of the theater's air conditioning, and they didn't stand up until the house lights came on. Ted stretched, something he always needed to do after sitting for any extended time, as Emma picked up their cups and the popcorn bucket, empty except for the kernels that hadn't popped. They walked up the aisle, Emma throwing the trash in the bin as a teenager dressed in a formal usher uniform made his way to the front with broom and dustpan in hand.

"Decent," Emma said as they stepped out into the lobby.

"Yes, but what was with all those quick cuts and explosions? And did the music have to be so loud?"

"You're sounding like an old man," Emma teased.

"I feel like an old man," Ted said with a smile.

The manager waved to them from behind the counter, popping fresh popcorn for the next show, and they waved back as they stepped out of the theater doors and into the blinding sunlight. The downtown sidewalks swirled with activity as people tried to squeeze in one more day of summer shopping and eating.

"Why do you think Mom did it?" Emma said as she put on her sunglasses.

"Did what?"

"You know, slash that guy's tires."

Ted stopped walking, stunned. "You think Mom did that?"

"Come on, you know her temper better than anyone."

The accusation came as a shock, not because it was outrageous, but because Emma figured it out before he had. Ted honestly thought it was either himself in drunken revelry or the group of teenagers, but not once thought it could have been Sophie. But the more he let the idea float around, the more weight it carried. The image of Sophie driving past midnight out to the edge of town, a sharp knife from the shop lying on the passenger seat in waiting, became concrete in his mind.

"Ted!" a voice called out.

He turned to see Marc Parker walking his way, his young son by his side. They hadn't spoken since the embarrassing incident at the park, and Ted hoped he wouldn't bring it up in front of Emma. The banker, dressed in a crisp denim shirt and blue jeans, greeted him and Emma with handshakes.

"Hi, Greg," Emma said as she crouched down on one knee, giving the boy a hug. "Ready for school to start?"

"Not really," Greg said, staring shyly at the sidewalk.

"How's college life treating you?" Marc asked Emma.

"Great, Mr. Parker," she answered as she stood back up. "Enjoying it very much."

"I remember my time at State. Some of the best times of my life." For several minutes, Marc talked about his college years. Emma smiled and nodded with recognition as the banker reminisced about football games, the late-night hot spots, and the different dormitories on campus. Their shared experience made Ted bittersweet, having missed out on college life himself but happy for Emma to enjoy it all.

Marc turned to Ted and placed a firm hand on his shoulder. "Remember that good news I mentioned a while back?"

"I do."

A businesslike smile spread over the mayor's face. "It's pure speculation at this point, and I don't want to get your hopes up just yet. But it may be excellent news, indeed."

"That sounds intriguing," Emma said.

"I'll stop by the shop as soon as I know more," Marc said as he took his son's hand. "But we better finish our back-to-school shopping or Mother's not going to be happy with us."

"Sure," Ted said.

"And Emma, wishing you all the best. If you ever need anything, just let me know. I should have some pull with all the money I give to the Alumni Association."

"Thanks, Mr. Parker." Emma looked down at Greg. "And after you're done shopping, stop by for some ice cream. On the house."

A smile broke across the young boy's face. "Can we, Dad?"

"If we get our shopping done fast," Marc said. "I know trying on clothes all afternoon isn't that much fun, but if we hurry with no complaining, we'll have time."

"I won't complain, promise!"

"Thank you," Marc said to both. "We'll stop by later this afternoon."

"Looking forward to it," Ted said.

Marc smiled and led Greg down the sidewalk, the boy looking over his shoulder and waving.

"Same old Mr. Parker," Emma said as she waved back. "Things never change around here."

After they stepped into the drugstore to pick up Sophie's prescription, Ted bought them both a can of cold soda from the vending machine. They drank from their cans as they strolled around the park. The Little League stands were empty, and the lush green grass now had scattered brown patches, a sure indication fall was on the horizon. They finished their sodas on the walking trail, threw their cans into the metal trash bins, and headed back to the shop.

Ted heard music in the distance as they turned the corner of the street. At the end of the block where Stroud's Ice Cream Shop stood, the *Lovely Rita* was parked. Several customers sat at the fold-out plastic table that lined the sidewalk near the truck while a small line of people waited at the truck's window to order.

"Oh no," Emma whispered. "I hope Mom hasn't seen this."

"Me too."

Ted followed Emma through the door of the shop to find Sophie standing at the counter, arms crossed and flashing a bitter smile.

"Do you see now?" she asked with a measured voice.

Ted nodded.

"What are you going to do about it?"

The thought of marching over to the *Lovely Rita* and challenging Brad to a fistfight flashed in his mind but the image was too silly. Ted thought of contacting the police; parking on a downtown street on a busy Saturday afternoon had to be a city code violation of some kind. But then a third alternative struck him, one that wouldn't involve violence or law enforcement.

"Emma," Ted said as he walked down the hallway toward the freezer. "Come help your old man."

He unlatched the freezer door as his daughter joined his side. The rush of frigid air soothed Ted as he grabbed the hand truck and rolled it over to a container of vanilla ice cream. Reading his mind, Emma lifted the box just enough for Ted to slide the base underneath. Ted lifted the container off the floor and wheeled it out into the hallway.

"Grabs some plastic bowls and spoons," Ted told Sophie as he pushed the ice cream past her. Emma jogged over and opened the door as he wheeled the container through and onto the sidewalk.

Across the street, two teenage boys slowly rode their bikes along the park trail and watched Ted with curiosity. He dropped the ice cream container down in front of the shop's window and motioned them over.

"Want some ice cream? It's on the house!"

Not believing their ears, the two boys gave each

other a look, checked for traffic, and walked their bikes across the street. Ted used his truck keys to pry off the lid of the container as Sophie and Emma joined him. Emma handed her father the metal scooper as Sophie handed the boys a bowl and spoon each. The ice cream was frozen solid, but Ted knew the heat would quickly solve that problem. After several attempts, he pushed the scooper through.

"Here you go," Ted said as he dropped the scoops into their bowls. "And make sure to tell all your friends. It'll be free as long as it lasts."

"We will!" the boys promised before digging into their unexpected summer treat.

Ted turned to the playground full of children and their parents. "Free ice cream! Hurry before it melts away!"

In what seemed only a matter of seconds, a small parade of parents leading their children from the playground appeared. Ted worried for a moment about traffic, but the parents made sure to hold their children's hands and used the crosswalk, and before long, a line formed along the sidewalk.

An older man out for a walk on the park trail stopped in his tracks, trying to figure out what was going on before crossing the street. Several women carrying department store shopping bags joined the queue as things began to work like an assembly line. Ted placed a scoop in the bowl Emma held out, and after Sophie added a spoon, she would hand the ice cream to the next person in line with a smile.

"Can I have some?" a shy girl around high school age asked when she reached the front of the line. "Or are we too old?"

"No one's too old for ice cream," Ted said as he handed her a bowl.

The girl smiled, and while holding the bowl with one hand and her phone with another, snapped a photo of her ice cream. The two boys on bikes returned with a group of friends following on them. One of the boys pointed toward Ted as they stopped and parked their bikes along the curb.

"I told you!" the pointing boy shouted as the others got in line.

Ted's hand started to cramp but he ignored the pain. The buzz of conversation drowned out the music from down the street, and the crowd reminded him of a time a few years ago when a small fire broke out in one of the abandoned downtown buildings. There was little damage, the firefighters snuffing out the fire with little trouble, but the large gathering of spectators that magically appeared from nowhere had amazed him.

A tall, shadowy figure from the *Lovely Rita* stepped out of the truck from down the street. Ted shielded his eyes with his hand and saw Brad Wilkinson standing still, arms crossed against his chest, and watching the activity in front of the ice cream shop. Ted made eye contact and shrugged his shoulders, but the only reaction Brad offered was letting his arms fall and stepping back inside.

A young mother held her little boy's hand as they reached the front. The sling that crossed her chest held a tiny infant with its face flushed from the heat. Ted scooped up a double serving as the boy's eyes lit up.

"Be sure to share with your mother," Ted said as Emma handed the boy the bowl.

"I will."

"What do we say?" the mother asked the boy.

"Thank you," the boy said without taking his eyes off the ice cream.

"You're most welcome," Emma said with a smile.

Thirty minutes later, the heat had turned the vanilla ice cream left into creamy milk. Ted would've loved to continue the battle, but that would only lead to losing more money in the long run. He had made his point; taking away business from his competitor for a brief time was victory enough.

"Sorry, everyone," Ted called out to the people left in line. "We're completely out of free ice cream for the day. But we have plenty inside, along with air conditioning, so please join us if you can."

The crowd let out a collective groan, some walking away, but several followed them inside, the promise of cool, refreshing ice cream on a hot summer day too tempting to ignore.

Growing up, Ted's mother always told him to be careful what he wished for. During the unbearable summer heat, Ted silently wished for fall weather to return as quickly as possible. But now with Thanksgiving in the recent past and Christmas on the horizon, his mother's advice came back to haunt him with the forecast of an unprecedented snowstorm headed their way.

In Howell, it snowed once or maybe twice a year, usually nothing more than a few inches of accumulation that quickly melted away the next day. But for the past week, weather forecasters encouraged viewers to stock up on all essential supplies and predicted at least a foot of snow. Mother Nature seemed very angry with their part of the world.

Ted drove carefully down the highway, the pavement already slick from a thin layer of ice. He hated driving at night with the heavy traffic trying to beat out the storm and gripped the steering wheel tight. Outside the windshield, one headlight burned brighter than the other as the thin, worn wipers tried their best to slash away the sleet.

The megastore lights lit up the distant sky, and Ted breathed a sigh of relief as he took the next exit off the highway. Meandering cars searched the parking lot for the closest spot to the entrance. Not wanting the hassle, Ted parked the truck at the far end of the lot, switched off the engine and lights, and took a deep breath. He slowly swung out of the truck, stepped onto the pavement with his heavy boots, and carefully walked toward the store. The automatic doors swished open when he reached them.

Packed with customers like him who waited to prepare for the storm, Ted regretted not visiting the store earlier in the week and grabbed a squeaky cart from the corral. Though well stocked himself on essentials, he discovered as he walked down the aisles that the store was low on coffee, eggs, and milk, and Ted didn't want to think about having to sacrifice them for the duration of the storm.

"Hey, ice cream man!" a voice called out. Still wearing the work vest of his father's hardware store, Frank's son George waved to him with one hand and held a plastic basket of groceries in the other. Ted hadn't seen the young man for some time, and he seemed older, his hair thinner and face fuller.

"Don't tell my dad you saw me here," George said as he walked over and offered his hand. Ted shook it. 'How's the family? Dad says Emma seems to be enjoying college life."

"We're doing good, and Frank's right. She's enjoying her time away from her parents very much."

Ted hesitated to elaborate further. His daughter had returned for the Thanksgiving break and brought along her boyfriend, a reserved and sober young man studying engineering. Aaron's attitude was the exact opposite of Emma's happy-go-lucky one, the epitome of *opposites attract*. From the numerous phone conversations between mother and daughter, Sophie shared her belief that the relationship was serious, and with Emma introducing the young man at a family holiday, Ted reached the same conclusion.

"Well, tell everyone hello from me," George said.

"Will do, and you do the same."

"Stay safe out there," George said over his shoulder and returned to his shopping.

Ted managed to scavenge a few cans of vegetable soup off the nearly empty shelf. Thinking homemade chili would be perfect for a snowy day, he fought against the swarm of other shoppers and went to the produce section and found several tomatoes and onions. Most of the chili seasoning was gone, though, and he settled for a couple of wrapped packets in the clearance section he hoped would work.

The checkout lines were long and loud, and feeling no urgency to get back out in the cold, Ted decided to see the rest of the store. In the past he only visited for a quick run of necessary groceries, but he was surprised when he came to a sporting goods section at the very back of the store. In Texas, fishing was a yearlong activity with the mostly warm weather, and Ted made a mental wish list as he walked down the aisle of hooks, rods, and reels.

"Don't touch my cart!" a woman shrieked in a raspy voice.

An older woman pointed an accusing finger at a teenager at the end of the aisle. The young man smirked, as if the woman wasn't even there.

"I said don't touch my cart!"

"I can't get through with you blocking up the whole aisle," the teenager said dismissively.

"My purse is in that cart!"

"Why do I care?"

"You might steal it!" she shouted even louder.

Ted thought of waving down an employee, but the teenager merely shook his head, picked up the item he needed from the shelf, and pushed his cart away. Trembling with rage, the woman gave Ted a look as if to say *Can you believe young people today?*

He merely shrugged in reply.

Ever since the November presidential election, Ted sensed the world becoming meaner. Other than fulfilling his voting duty every four years, he didn't care much for politics. Every passing election gave him the knowledge that whoever won, whether he supported them or not, would do things he both agreed and disagreed with. But this election seemed different, as if the fragile bridge between the two opposing political parties had fallen into the water below. He hoped the constant bickering that seeped through the presidential race would have ended, the country returning to a semblance of normality for the next four years, but Ted thought it more unlikely with every passing day.

He picked up a blanket and a couple of fluffy pillows as he pushed his way toward the checkout lanes. They didn't necessarily need them, but it felt good not to worry about money for a moment.

Marc Parker had visited the ice cream shop in August and revealed that an investment group was interested in purchasing several downtown buildings to convert into apartments. With business and housing expansion headed toward the highway, Marc explained, downtown Howell needed to be revitalized. Ted knew the real reason for the investors' interest was that downtown property was relatively cheap. With the town's population expanding, converting affordable buildings into living spaces could offer a nice long-term profit margin.

At first, Ted believed he'd decline any offer. He couldn't imagine living without the biggest part of his family's heritage. But when Marc scribbled down a monetary figure on a napkin and slid it to him, Ted's world became surreal. Though not a large number for a bank or a typical business, the offer was more than Ted thought he could save in a lifetime. Marc registered his shock and told him to relax, a decision didn't need to be made immediately, and to take some time to consider and discuss with Sophie and Emma.

Later that evening, as Ted and Sophie sat at the

kitchen table, he took out the napkin and unfolded it, laying it down on the table. He explained the details as his wife's eyes grew wide. With Emma's college tuition a growing concern, the offer made the three remaining years of her education and a frugal but comfortable retirement possible. They hadn't reached a definite decision by bedtime, but when Ted awoke the next morning, he stepped into the kitchen to see Sophie with a big smile on her face.

"Let's do it," she said. "I couldn't sleep last night thinking about it."

"Maybe we should talk with Emma first," Ted said.

Sophie looked at her coffee cup, circling the tip of her finger around its edge. "Emma's living her own life now, Ted."

Deep down he had secretly entertained the thought of his daughter carrying on the family business but knew his wife was right. Strangely there was a part of him that felt relief that she didn't have to follow in her father's footsteps that didn't lead anywhere. Ted knew Emma would scratch out her own life, with both the hurt and the joy the world offered, and hoped for nothing but the best.

"But you have to promise something," Sophie said.

"What's that?"

"You must get some type of job. I can't have you moping around the house all day. I might have to kill you after a month or two."

Ted smiled, knowing that if Sophie was exaggerating, it wasn't by much.

After a hearty breakfast, he put on his best suit and tie and drove to the downtown bank. The clerk welcomed Ted warmly and led him inside the office of Marc Parker, who waited for him with an open hand. They both sat down to discuss the offer, but suddenly second thoughts swirled in his mind. Was he betraying his family legacy? But as the president of the bank dived into the numbers, Ted thought of how proud his father would be to have known that his business had seen three generations and was worth more than he could've possibly imagined. All summer Ted felt as if he was drowning, and here was Marc Paker throwing him a lifebuoy to grab onto.

Ted's wandering mind snapped back to the present when he reached the checkout lanes. The lines stretched out down the aisles and Ted pushed his cart to the line closest to him. He watched customer after customer unloading their items almost in a trance, time moving slow, until he finally found himself face-to-face with the bored cashier. Ted had fewer groceries than most, and by the time a sacker had hustled over, the cashier had scanned and sacked the items herself. Ted paid with his credit card, the cashier handed over his receipt, and he led the sacker pushing his cart of bagged groceries toward the exit.

"They should pay you guys extra working on

nights like this," Ted said over his shoulder.

"No such luck," the young man said, his voice muffled by a heavy scarf wrapped around his neck. "But the boss says it might snow so much we won't be able to open tomorrow. A day off would be nice."

The wind had picked up since Ted had entered the store, and the harsh parking lot lights illuminated heavy snowflakes falling from the sky. Ice had begun to form on the windshields of the parked cars as he took out his keys.

"You can hand them to me," Ted said when they reached his truck and opened the passenger door.

The young man nodded as reached in and picked up a full sack and handed it over. Even though he'd been outside for only a minute or two, Ted hurriedly placed the last sack on the floorboard as the cold swept over him.

"Have a good night," the young man said, turning the shopping cart back toward the store.

"You too. And stay warm."

Ted carefully stepped around the truck and opened the driver's side door, climbing inside. He turned the key and let the engine warm for a minute before he turned on the defroster. The gathering ice on the windshield was slow to melt, and Ted hoped the wipers would help scratch them off, but they only made harsh screeching sounds with every slash. The headlights flickered several times when he flipped the switch before kicking in, the engine making a new rumbling sound.

"Just please get me home," Ted muttered under his breath.

The weak defroster and windshield wipers were losing the battle to the ice and snow. Ted leaned over and popped open the glove compartment, rifling through registration papers, small tools, and his hidden cigars in search of an ice scraper. Coming up empty, he assumed he'd left it in Sophie's car sometime last winter, and after a few more sweeps of the wipers across the glass, shut off the engine. He took a deep breath, not wanting to brave the store another time, but didn't want to gamble on driving down the highway with limited visibility.

The swirling wind beat against him as Ted walked toward the entrance. He watched a car looking for a parking spot lose traction and slide helplessly toward a light pole before the driver gained control at the last second and avoided the crash. When he reached the automatic doors, he happened to turn to his right to see a tall woman in a heavy parka standing by the vending machines, smoking a cigarette and staring off toward the highway.

"Rita?" Ted asked.

The woman looked up as she brought the cigarette down to her side. Under her unbuttoned parka, Ted saw that she wore the bright yellow uniform of the megastore. "Oh, Mr. Stroud. How are you doing tonight?"

Ted stuffed his cold, ungloved hands in his coat pockets and walked over to her. "Good, other than realizing I'm the only driver in Howell tonight without an ice scraper."

Rita smiled. "You won't find one in that madhouse. I think we sold the last one early this morning."

"Just my luck," Ted said.

"Mr. Stroud . . ."

"Call me Ted."

"Ted. Could I talk with you for a moment?"

"Sure."

Rita motioned to the empty bench by the vending machines. "Please, sit down. I can put this out if it bothers you."

"No, don't do that," Ted said as he sat. "I love the smell of cigarettes, especially in cold weather."

Rita smiled and took a long drag before she exhaled a stream of smoke into the night. "Would you like one?" she asked as she sat down next to him.

Ted shook his head. "Better not. Promised my wife I'd wouldn't pick up the habit again."

"I understand," Rita said. "I don't smoke often, but sometimes a good cigarette clears my head." She motioned toward the store entrance with people rushing in and out.

"I didn't know you worked here."

"Yeah, but just temporarily. The summer profits didn't last as long as we hoped for. Brad had a tough time finding anything but substitute teaching, so here I am. Got to do what you got to do." She tossed her cigarette to the slush on the sidewalk where the flame sizzled out.

"Sorry to hear that. Our summer wasn't that great, either."

Rita's eyes grew wide. "Oh, shit! Here I'm complaining when you guys closed your shop."

Ted grinned. "Let's just say we had an offer we couldn't refuse."

Rita studied his eyes. "Is that a good thing or a bad thing?"

Ted turned and watched the cars and trucks moving across the highway. "Good question. We've been struggling the past few years, so it's for the best. Sometimes you must read the writing on the wall. But finding something new to do at my age is giving me second thoughts."

"Come on, Mr. Stroud. You're not that old."

"You're too kind, Rita."

Rita placed a hand on his shoulder. "There's something I've been meaning to talk to you about. Remember when our tires got slashed?"

Ted nodded. "Of course."

"Well, I feel so ashamed, but I was convinced it was you. Brad didn't think so, but I gradually convinced him. My husband, to put it bluntly, is too nice of a guy. Never wants to rock the boat. I told him he needed to confront you about it, and I guess I wore him down. It was probably one of the hardest things he's ever done."

"That's all water under the bridge," was all Ted could think of saying.

"But we did find out who slashed the tires."

"Really?" Ted said with a nervous laugh, still convinced it was Sophie.

"We live in this new development. Lot of construction with the new houses going up. This group of kids hang around the neighborhood at night, drinking and smoking, harmless stuff. Sometimes Brad goes over and talks to them. He's not much older than them, anyways. More of a big brother than a father figure. They can talk stuff with him that they might not have anyone else to share their thoughts with."

"Understood," Ted said.

"A fire broke out in one of the recently built frame structures a few nights after our tires were slashed. We were sitting around watching television when we smelled smoke. None of our alarms were going off, so we stepped outside and saw the flames down the street. It was quite a sight, and luckily far enough away not to be any danger to any of the other houses."

"That's good."

"Other than the foundation being seared and the structure burnt to a crisp, the damage was minimal. The construction company was sure angry, though."

"I bet."

"One construction guy came by after our little ice cream battle on Main Street. Our next-door neighbor had installed security cameras on their property and gave him their video footage. This guy knocked on our door one day and showed us some photos from the video. For the most part, they were blurry, but Brad recognized a few faces. He told the guy he didn't know any of them, but we found out later the kids were picked up and questioned by the police. I've never seen my husband so heartbroken in his life. He never thought those kids could be so destructive, and if they could do that, slashing a few tires wasn't that big of a deal."

Though not totally convinced, Ted nodded in agreement. Rita took out her pack of cigarettes, her hands trembling from the cold as she pulled one out, a frigid wind whipping around them.

"I need one more before my break's over. You sure you don't want one?"

Ted quickly glanced around him to see if there were any familiar faces. "Okay, just one."

Rita smiled as she held out the pack. He gently slid a cigarette out and placed it in the corner of his mouth. She offered the flame from her lighter and Ted inhaled deeply, the smoke warming his lungs.

"He thought he was helping those kids," Rita said as she snapped her lighter shut. "In addition to being too nice, he's incredibly trusting."

"Need more people like that in the world," Ted

said.

"Maybe so. But I wanted to apologize to you."

"No need for that. Hell, I would've reached the same conclusion."

Rita nodded, and they smoked their cigarettes in silence and watched the snow fall. The highway traffic had thinned considerably since Ted had arrived at the store and he wondered how hazardous the drive back home might be. Rita took one last inhale, looked at her watch, and tossed the cigarette onto the slushy sidewalk.

"Well, back to the monkey house," she said. "I'm glad we had a chance to talk."

"Anytime. I'm used to saying stop by the shop but will have to try to quit that habit. Maybe something civilized like dinner and a movie."

Rita stood up and smiled. "I'd like that. We'd like that."

Rita crossed her arms over her chest and gave Ted a tiny wave as the automatic doors opened and she stepped inside. Ted sat there for a few more moments, savoring the taboo cigarette before dropping it with the others in the slush.

Ted bought a plastic spatula in the store and took it out to the truck. After warming up the engine and running the defroster at full power, he placed the edge of the spatula on the thin sheet of ice on the windshield. The handle bent and threatened to snap with each scrape, but after a few minutes, the ice melted enough that he was able to clear the windshield. He did the same for the rear window and, when done, stuffed the worn spatula in the full trash can next to the cart corral. He climbed into the truck, the cabin now warmed up and comfortable, and slowly reversed out of the parking space.

The cigarette and the cold gave Ted a thirst for his glovebox cigars. He had finished the first cigar when he took the highway exit ramp that led home. While the highway traffic was slow, the downtown streets were empty. Sleet crunched under the tires as snowflakes twinkled in the headlights, and with no other cars around, the sidewalks and streets were covered with sparkling pristine snow.

He took a right turn onto Main Street. Since the sale of the building, Ted had avoided driving in downtown Howell. Even the thought of driving by the ice cream shop filled him with anxiety, believing that the wave of nostalgia would be overwhelming, but the winter weather compelled him. Other than a few small dustings of snowfall through the years, Ted couldn't remember a time downtown looked so picturesque.

The light flashed red at the intersection, but not seeing any other traffic around, Ted drove slowly through and brought the truck to a stop against the curb. The howling wind struck his face as he rolled down the engine and tossed the lit cigar to the street. He braced himself for the cold, shut off the engine, and opened the door and stepped outside.

The unlit neon store sign still hung above the doors, the snow accumulating on top of it. Ted walked over to the large window where *Stroud's Ice Cream Shop* was stenciled with decorative flair and peered inside. The streetlights gave just enough light for him to see the bare walls and dusty checkerboard-tiled floor. All the birthday photos were gone, the tables and chairs bought and taken away, and the kitchen equipment sold. The only remnant of the shop Ted still owned was the jukebox that now sat in the corner of his living room, taking up way too much space.

Stroud's Ice Cream Shop officially closed the Saturday before Labor Day. After a summer of barely turning a profit, and with the offer for the building way more than Ted had anticipated, the decision was simple. Ted and Sophie invited the entire town to stop by for one last scoop of ice cream and to feel free to take framed photographs of family members from the walls. He fed the jukebox with enough quarters to keep the music playing all day long and took the opportunity of every break to dance with Sophie slowly across the room.

Over the next few months they sold most of the furnishings and equipment at auction. As Ted watched everything being hauled away, he felt pangs of guilt, but Sophie reassured him that his father would've made the same choice. Ted wasn't convinced; his father had always been strong and weathered every storm.

As he stood at the window, the expected sting of melancholy of days gone by failed to come. The dark, empty dining room added nothing to the memories already etched securely in his mind. Ted tried not to think of the uncertain future but felt a small sense of contentment in his place in the world.

Ted took one more glance around the bare room and noticed that the shopkeeper's bell still hung above the door. A part of him regretted forgetting to take it down and bring it home. The deep, metallic clang was the first sound he heard when he unlocked the door and the last when he turned off the lights at the end of the day. But then he thought that maybe it was a good thing and hoped the new owner wouldn't take it down, the clang of the bell serving as an echo from the past.

Ted pushed his cold hands in his pockets and turned away from the window. Across the street the small hills and trees in the park covered in the snow looked like something out of a Christmas card. He climbed back in the truck and turned the key. The engine struggled back to life, the weak headlight fading in and out before brightening fully.

Ted shifted into drive. The wheels spun helplessly in the snow for several seconds before finding traction, and he pulled the truck away from the curb and followed the headlights home.

Acknowledgements

Very special thanks to Chad Duerksen and Joe Douglas Trent for reading and sharing their thoughts on the early drafts of this story. Also special thanks to Christie Perlmutter and Ryan Schumacher for their review; their suggestions improved this story immensely. And "shout outs" to the Caprock Writers' and Illustrators' Alliance and the Write Right Critique Group of Lubbock for their tremendous support.

The book you hold in your hand wouldn't exist without the tremendous work and creativity of Hannah Gaskamp. I am so grateful and hope my words can live up to her wonderful cover and design.

About the Author

John A. Brock lives and writes in Lubbock, Texas. Connect with him on Instagram at @jabrockwrites or at jabrockwrites@gmail.com